YO HO HO!

MARJORIE NEWMAN

Illustrated by Kate Sheppard

www.randomhousechildrens.co.uk

For Anna

YO HO HO
A CORGI BOOK 978 0 552 56897 5

Published in Great Britain by Corgi Books,
an imprint of Random House Children's Publishers UK
A Random House Group Company

Corgi Pups edition published 1996
This Colour First Reader edition published 2013

1 3 5 7 9 10 8 6 4 2

The Random House Group Limited supports the Forest Stewardship Council (FSC®),
the leading international forest certification organization. Our books carrying the FSC
label are printed on FSC®-certified paper. FSC is the only forest certification scheme
endorsed by the leading environmental organizations, including Greenpeace. Our paper
procurement policy can be found at www.randomhouse.co.uk/environment.

MIX
Paper from
responsible sources
FSC® C013123
FSC
www.fsc.org

Set in Bembo MT Schoolbook 21/28pt

Corgi Books are published by Random House Children's Publishers UK,
61–63 Uxbridge Road, London W5 5SA

www.**randomhousechildrens**.co.uk
www.**randomhouse**.co.uk

Addresses for companies within The Random House Group Limited can be found at:
www.randomhouse.co.uk/offices.htm

THE RANDOM HOUSE GROUP Limited Reg. No. 954009

A CIP catalogue record for this book is available from the British Library.

Printed in Italy.

Contents

COLOUR FIRST READER books are perfect for beginner readers. All the text inside this Colour First Reader book has been checked and approved by a reading specialist, so it is the ideal size, length and level for children learning to read.

Series Reading Consultant: Prue Goodwin
Honorary Fellow of the University of Reading

Chapter One

"This is Mr Cutlass," said Mrs Smith, the headmistress. "He is your new teacher."

Class 4 looked at their new teacher. He wasn't like the other teachers. He wore a spotted scarf round his neck. And he had a parrot on his shoulder.

"What's the parrot's name?" asked Oko.

"Nipper," said Mr Cutlass.

"We don't usually have pets in school," frowned Mrs Smith. "Mr Cutlass says Nipper will help with lessons."

"Ar. That he will," said Mr Cutlass.

Class 4 laughed. Mr Cutlass laughed, too. Nipper squawked, and flapped his wings.

Mrs Smith did not laugh.

"I hope everything will be all right," she said. She walked out of the room.

Mr Cutlass winked at Class 4.

"Right, mates! The first lesson is singing!"

He began to sing a loud sea song. Soon everyone in the room was singing loud sea songs. Nipper squawked, and flapped his wings.

"He's helping!" said Mr Cutlass. Class 4 laughed.

Lessons were fun now. Mr Cutlass had lots of good ideas. Besides, Nipper sat on the children's shoulders. They liked that.

But if they were rough, Mr Cutlass cried, "Watch it, mate! Or you'll have to walk the plank!"

Some of the little children
didn't know what he meant. But
Class 4 knew. They remembered
stories they had heard. The stories
were about pirates . . .

Sometimes the other teachers looked hard at Mr Cutlass. Sometimes Mrs Smith, the headteacher, looked very hard at Mr Cutlass. The school got a new caretaker, called Mr Jones. He looked very hard at Mr Cutlass, too.

But no-one asked, "Are you a pirate, Mr Cutlass?"

Even Mrs Smith didn't ask. She was afraid it might seem rude.

Soon everyone began to get used to Mr Cutlass and Nipper. Most people forgot about pirates.

But Class 4 didn't forget.

And the school caretaker watched Mr Cutlass closely . . .

One day, the wind blew hard around the school. Mr Cutlass looked out of the window, and sighed.

He taught Class 4 a new sea song. The song was soft, and sad. "Ar. I used to sing that song," he sighed. "With the ship rocking on the waves . . . the wind blowing through the sails . . . Ar."

Class 4 looked at one another.

"Mr Cutlass," said James, "were you ever a – sailor?"

"Ar. That I was," sighed Mr Cutlass.

"Mr Cutlass," whispered Mary. "Were you ever a – pirate?"

Class 4 held its breath.

Chapter Two

Mr Cutlass looked at Class 4.

"Can you keep a secret, mates?" he asked.

"Yes!" cried Class 4.

"Then I'll tell you. I was once a pirate. Captain Cutlass. That was me."

Class 4 shivered with excitement.

"Why did you stop?" asked Ranjit.

"It's wrong to be a pirate," said Mr Cutlass. "So I gave it up."

"Did you find a lot of treasure?" asked Mary.

"I did," smiled Mr Cutlass.

"Did you have a brave pirate crew?" asked Taki.

"I did!" smiled Mr Cutlass.

"Did you have lots of fights?" asked Jill.

"Lots!" smiled Mr Cutlass. "Especially with Dastardly Dan. He was my sworn enemy. Many a time we've had a desperate battle. I always won. But only just . . ."

Class 4 shivered again. Nipper
squawked and flapped his wings.
"Ar," said Mr Cutlass. "Old
Nipper knows all about it!"
"Tell us!" begged Class 4.

"Please, Mr Cutlass!"

"Well—" began Mr Cutlass.
That day, and every day,
Mr Cutlass told them pirate
stories.

Dastardly Dan was in every story. He was a big ugly man. He had a wickedly flashing gold tooth which showed when he smiled.

Dastardly Dan sank every ship
he came across. He only rescued
the sailors if they paid him lots of
money. Even then he didn't take
them back to port. He left them
on desert islands. He was always

making one of his crew walk the plank, especially when his ship was sailing through crocodile-infested water. And he had an evil laugh. "Har har har har har!"

Class 4 shivered.

One day, Mr Cutlass
whispered, "Class 4 – would you
like to see a secret message?"

"Oh, yes please!" they cried.

Mr Cutlass pulled a piece of
paper from his pocket. Class 4
crowded round to look.

"A friend gave it to me," said Mr Cutlass. "It's about hidden treasure. I've never bothered to work it out."

"We'll work it out!" cried Class 4.

"All right," said Mr Cutlass.
"But remember! I'm not a pirate
now. So we won't look for the
treasure. And you must keep all
this very secret. Because—"

He stopped.

"Because what?" cried Class 4.

"Because Dastardly Dan knows I have the message!" whispered Mr Cutlass. "If he should come after us . . ."

Class 4 shivered. "We'll keep it very secret!" they promised. They didn't like the sound of Dastardly Dan and his wickedly flashing gold tooth.

They tried to work out what
the message meant.

Chapter Three

Class 4 looked at the message for a very long time.

"That's a rock," said Oko.

"And that's a stone," said Mary. "Rock. Stone. Trees . . ."

"The trees mean a wood!" cried Taki. "Rock-stone Wood! That's not very far away!"

"A white house!"
cried Jenny. "By a pond!"
"White-house Pond!"
cried Class 4.

"That's the pond in
Rock-stone Wood!"
"Well done,
mates!" said Mr
Cutlass. "I'd never
have known that."

"These marks are footprints!" said Pat. "We must take five steps to the east."

"Then three steps to the south!" said Liz.

"Then we must dig for treasure!" cried everyone.

"So we must!" cried Mr
Cutlass. Then he stopped. "But
I'm not a pirate now," he said.
"We're not going to look for
treasure. And none of you can go
on your own!" he added. "You
promised to keep this a secret. So
you can't ask your grown-ups to
take you."

Class 4 were very, very
disappointed.

They got on with their work.
But the room was sad. Nipper
didn't squawk. He didn't flap his
wings. Everything was very quiet.

Until—

"Mr Cutlass!" cried Jill. "We
could give the treasure to the
school fund!"

"Yes! Yes!" cried Class 4.

Mr Cutlass thought hard. Then he smiled. "Ar!" he said. "I guess that wouldn't be wrong."

"Hooray!" cried Class 4. Nipper squawked, and flapped his wings.

No-one knew the school caretaker had heard the cheering. No-one knew he'd crept up to listen outside the classroom door . . .

"Hold hard, Class 4," said Mr Cutlass. "We can't look for treasure. It's not on the school timetable."

Class 4 were quiet.

Until—

"It could be a school trip!" James cried. "We could go pond dipping for our Nature topic!"

"Yes! Yes!" cried Class 4.

The caretaker was puzzled. How would pond dipping find treasure?

But Class 4 all cheered. Nipper squawked loudly.

Mr Cutlass held up his hand. Class 4 was quiet. Was Mr Cutlass going to say 'No'?

Chapter Four

"Class 4," said Mr Cutlass. "We will make it a school trip!"

Everyone cheered again. They were very excited.

The caretaker went to make a telephone call . . .

It was hard for Class 4 to keep
their secret. But they managed it.
No-one said 'treasure' again until
they were in the coach, on their
way to Rock-stone wood.

Then Mr Cutlass told
everything to the mums who had
come with them.

The mums were very excited.

No-one noticed a car
following the coach . . .

The coach stopped at Rock-
stone Wood. The car stopped just
down the road. The caretaker
and his brother sneaked out of
the car. Three other men sneaked
out of the car.

The children walked to White-
house Pond. They did some pond
dipping.

At last Mr Cutlass thought
Class 4 had done enough work.

"Right, mates!" he said.

The mums and children held
their breath. Mr Cutlass went
to the corner of the pond. He
stepped five steps to the east.
Then he stepped three steps to
the south.

Then he said, "Dig!"

The children rushed forwards.
They all helped to dig.

Presently their spades hit
something hard!

Mr Cutlass bent down to
look. "It's a wooden box!" he
whispered.

Everyone helped to dig out the box. But as they lifted it up, the box split. Treasure fell out on to the grass!

"Hooray!" yelled the children and the mums and Mr Cutlass.

"Wheeee!" came another shout.
Up rushed the caretaker and his
brother and the others. Nipper
squawked, and flapped his wings.

"It's Dastardly Dan!" shouted
Mr Cutlass.

"Dastardly Dan's my brother!" cried the caretaker. "My name isn't Jones! I've been spying on you all the time, Cutlass!"

"Quick!" cried Class 4. "Save the treasure!"

The children and the mums
grabbed it up. The enemy pirates
grabbed, as well. Dastardly Dan
yelled as he grabbed. His long
arms seemed to be everywhere.
But the children were better at
grabbing. They were closer to
the ground. They got in amongst

the pirates. They stamped on the
pirates' toes. They pulled the pirates'
long hair. Nipper flapped and
squawked and pecked. And Mr
Cutlass seized Dastardly Dan from
behind and crashed him to the
ground.

Then—

"Back to the coach!" yelled
Mr Cutlass.

The children and the mums
rushed for the coach, carrying
the treasure. The pirates came

after them, yelling because of their sore toes. Dastardly Dan was up on his feet – he was chasing Mr Cutlass – he was almost catching him!

Then Nipper squawked, and
flapped his wings in Dastardly
Dan's face. It gave Mr Cutlass
just time to reach the coach.

The coach started up. Mr
Cutlass was pulled on in the nick
of time. Nipper
flew in at the
open window.

The coach sped down the road.
Dastardly Dan and his crew ran
for their car. They gave chase.

Along the roads sped the coach,
with the car behind it.

The coach sounded its horn.
Nipper squawked, and flapped his
wings. The children cheered and
shouted. The mums
cheered and shouted.

Mr Cutlass cheered and
shouted.

The pirates just shouted.

The car was getting closer . . .
closer . . . It was almost catching
up . . .

Would the coach reach the
school in time? Would Mrs Smith
and the others come out to help?

Then the children heard a
Police siren. A Police car was
chasing them.

Dastardly Dan and his crew
were frightened of the Police.
They turned off at the next corner
and sped away.

The Police sent a radio message.
Another Police car would stop
Dastardly Dan for speeding.

The school coach slowed down,
and stopped.

The Police car stopped behind
it. Two big policemen got out.
They walked up to the coach.

Chapter Five

Everyone began to talk at once.
Nipper squawked, and flapped
his wings.

"Quiet!" yelled the policemen.

Everyone was quiet.

"Now, sir," said the policemen.
"What's been going on?"

Mr Cutlass explained everything. "We were only speeding to get away from Dastardly Dan," he finished. "We're very sorry. We'll never do it again."

"What a story!" smiled the policemen. "It's a pity," they added, "but it's the law here that treasure trove doesn't belong to the person who finds it.

It belongs to the Crown. That's the Queen."

"What?" cried everyone. They were very upset.

It was true. The treasure did belong to the Crown. It went into a museum. But the school was paid a lot of money for it.

The story was in the
newspapers and on television.
Lots of people sent money to
help with the school fund.

Mrs Smith, and all the
teachers, and all the children, had
a great time spending the money.

The school got a new
caretaker. Dastardly Dan didn't
come back. And everyone said
Class 4 had the most exciting
teacher in the world.

Class 4 thought so, too!

THE END

Colour First Readers

Welcome to Colour First Readers. The following pages are intended for any adults (parents, relatives, teachers) who may buy these books to share the stories with youngsters. The pages explain a little about the different stages of learning to read and offer some suggestions about how best to support children at a very important point in their reading development.

Children start to learn about reading as soon as someone reads a book aloud to them when they are babies. Book-loving babies grow into toddlers who enjoy sitting on a lap listening to a story, looking at pictures or joining in with familiar words. Young children who have listened to stories start school with an expectation of enjoyment from books and this positive outlook helps as they are taught to read in the more formal context of school.

Cracking the code

Before they can enjoy reading for and to themselves, all children have to learn how to crack the alphabetic code and make meaning out of the lines and squiggles we call letters and punctuation. Some lucky pupils find the process of learning to read undemanding; some find it very hard.

Most children, within two or three years, become confident at working out what is written on the page. During this time they will probably read collections of books which are graded; that is, the books introduce a few new words and increase in length, thus helping youngsters gradually to build up their growing ability to work out the words and understand basic meanings.

Eventually, children will reach a crucial point when, without any extra help, they can decode words in an entire book, albeit a short one. They then enter the next phase of becoming a reader.

Making meaning

It is essential, at this point, that children stop seeing progress as gradually 'climbing a ladder' of books of ever-increasing difficulty. There is a transition stage between building word recognition skills and enjoying reading a story. Up until now, success has depended on getting the words right but to get pleasure from reading to themselves, children need to fully comprehend the content of what they read. Comprehension will only be reached if focus is put on understanding meaning and that can only happen if the reader is not hesitant when decoding. At this fragile, transition stage, decoding should be so easy that it slowly becomes automatic. Reading a book with ease enables children to get lost in the story, to enjoy the unfolding narrative at the same time as perfecting their newly learned word recognition skills.

At this stage in their reading development, children need to:

- Practice their newly established early decoding skills at a level which eventually enables them to do it automatically

- Concentrate on making sensible meanings from the words they decode

- Develop their ability to understand when meanings are 'between the lines' and other use of literary language

- Be introduced, very gradually, to longer books in order to build up stamina as readers

In other words, new readers need books that are well within their reading ability and that offer easy encounters with humour, inference, plot-twists etc. In the past, there have been very few children's books that provided children with these vital experiences at an early stage. Indeed, some children had to leap from highly controlled teaching materials to junior novels.

This experience often led to reluctance in youngsters who were not yet confident enough to tackle longer books.

Matching the books to reading development

Colour First Readers fill the gap between early reading and children's literature and, in doing so, support inexperienced readers at a vital time in their reading development. Reading aloud to children continues to be very important even after children have learned to read and, as they are well written by popular children's authors, Colour First Readers are great to read aloud. The stories provide plenty of opportunities for adults to demonstrate different voices or expression and, in a short time, give lots to talk about and enjoy together.

Each book in the series combines a number of highly beneficial features, including:

- Well-written and enjoyable stories by popular children's authors

- Unthreatening amounts of print on a page

- Unrestricted but accessible vocabularies

- A wide interest age to suit the different ages at which children might reach the transition stage of reading development

- Different sorts of stories – traditional, set in the past, present or future, real life and fantasy, comic and serious, adventures, mysteries etc.

- A range of engaging illustrations by different illustrators

- Stories which are as good to read aloud to children as they are to be read alone

All in all, Colour First Readers are to be welcomed for children throughout the early primary school years – not only for learning to read but also as a series of good stories to be shared by everyone. I like to think that the word 'Readers' in the title of this series refers to the many young children who will enjoy these books on their journey to becoming lifelong bookworms.

Prue Goodwin
Honorary Fellow of the University of Reading

Helping children to enjoy *Yo Ho Ho!*

If a child can read a page or two fluently, without struggling with the words at all, then he/she should be able to read this book alone. However, children are all different and need different levels of support to help them become confident enough to read a book to themselves.

Some young readers will not need any help to get going; they can just get on with enjoying the story. Others may lack confidence and need help getting into the story. For these children, it may help if you talk about what might happen in the book.

Explore the title, cover and first few illustrations with them, making comments and suggestions about any clues to what might happen in the story. Read the first chapter aloud together. Don't make it a chore. If they are still reluctant to do it alone, read the whole book with them, making it an enjoyable experience.

The following suggestions will not be necessary every time a book is read but, every so often, when a story has been particularly enjoyed, children love responding to it through creative activities.

Before reading

Yo Ho Ho! is a school story with a difference. Class 4 have a new teacher who turns out to be an ex-pirate called Mr Cutlass. Children may need to be reminded about pirates so that they can pick up the clues in the vocabulary (e.g. parrot, cutlass, walking the plank) and in the illustrations.

During reading

Asking questions about a story can be really helpful to support understanding but don't ask too many – and don't make it feel like test on what has happened. Relate the questions to the child's own experiences and imagination. For example, ask: 'Would you like to have an ex-pirate as your teacher?' or 'What do you think will be in the Treasure Chest?'

Responding to the book

If your child has enjoyed this story, it increases the fun by doing something creative in response. If possible, provide art materials and dressing up clothes so that they can make things, play at being characters, write and draw, act out a scene or respond in some other way to the story.

Activities for children

If you have enjoyed reading this story, you could:

• Make yourself a pirate outfit with dressing up clothes, bright scarves and an eye patch. Make a Jolly Roger flag with a black background and white skull and crossbones. Find a small box to make into a treasure chest. Look for bits of shiny paper and sweet wrappers to make into coins and jewels.

• Check the fun that Mr Cutlass had with his class. Does your teacher: sing sea songs; have a parrot; share secret messages about treasure; and, tell tales about being a pirate?

• Look at the picture on pages 24 & 25. Can you find:

1. **Dastardly Dan? [Who is Dastardly Dan's brother?]**

2. **Someone walking the plank? [Is he wearing a blindfold over his eyes?]**

3. **Crocodiles in the water? [How many?]**

4. **A sailor left on a desert island? [What else is on the island?]**

74

5. A Jolly Roger flag? [Have you made a flag yet?]

- Using pictures, make up a secret message about some hidden treasure. You could also draw a map of a treasure island.

- Do the *Yo Ho Ho!* Name Quiz:

  - **What is the headteacher's name?**

  - **What is the name of the parrot?**

  - **What is the name of Mr Cutlass's worst enemy?**

  - **Name four children in Class 4. (Clue: pages 33, 34 & 35)**

- Find a book about pirates in the library. Mr Cutlass said, 'It is wrong to be a pirate so I gave it up.' Look in the book to find out why being a pirate is wrong.

ALSO AVAILABLE AS COLOUR FIRST READERS